For Sienna —T.R.

randomhousekids.com

ISBN 978-0-7364-3598-7 (trade)
ISBN 978-0-7364-8184-7 (lib. bdg.)

Printed in the United States of America

10 9 8 7 6 5 4 3 2 1

Whisker Haven

TALES

with the

palace pets

A Midsummer Night's Dreamy

By Tennant Redbank

Illustrated by Rosa La Barbera,
Elisabetta Melaranci, and the Tomatofarm team

Random House 🏠 New York

"*Woof! Woof, woof, woof!*"

Dreamy was in the middle of the loveliest dream. It was about a forest in summer. There was a queen, a king . . . and a donkey? But the sound of barking chased her dream away.

She cracked open one eye. White fur flashed past. Her friend Pumpkin the puppy was dancing circles around her.

1

"Have you heard the news?" Pumpkin asked. "Whisker Haven is putting on a show!"

Dreamy rolled onto her back to see Pumpkin better. "What kind of show?"

"I don't know!" Pumpkin jumped away and spun around. "Sultan and I are going to town to find out. Want to come along?"

Dreamy considered for a moment.

Nope. She'd rather nap. Maybe her dream would return.

Dreamy loved to nap. It was her talent. Sure, she was a kindhearted kitten. She was clever, too. But when it came to sleep, Dreamy was a pro.

"*Woof!*" Pumpkin gave another excited bark.

Dreamy sat up and stretched from her front paws to her back paws. Actually, a walk with her friends *would* be nice. She could always nap later. "All right," she said.

Pumpkin ran to the front door of the Pawlace. Sultan the tiger cub was waiting for them.

"Ready to rock and roar?" Sultan asked.

"Let's go, let's go, let's go!" Pumpkin yapped.

Dreamy, Sultan, and Pumpkin walked into town. Or Dreamy walked while Pumpkin and Sultan chased each other along the path.

"We're almost there!" Sultan called. He and Pumpkin dashed back to Dreamy.

"I can't wait to hear about the show!" Pumpkin said.

The puppy and the tiger cub raced ahead again. And back again. By the time they neared the village, they had probably run twice as far as Dreamy.

And I'm twice as sleepy, Dreamy thought as they reached the first shops.

"Let's get treats at Mr. Chow's," Sultan said. He gave a little growl. Sultan loved Mr. Chow's tiger treats.

"And we can find out about the show!" Pumpkin said.

Dreamy spotted a flyer on the wall of Tillie's Tutu Tailor Shop. "Look at this," she said to her friends.

The Whisker Haven Players

present

A MIDSUMMER NIGHT'S DREAM

TRYOUTS TODAY!

"That's it," Pumpkin said. "That's the show!" She wagged her tail. "I want to be in it! Do you think I can be in it?"

"Who are the Whisker Haven Players?" Dreamy asked.

"The town's drama club," Sultan said. "They put on a show every summer. Any pet or Critterzen can try out."

"Maybe Tillie knows more," Dreamy said.

Dreamy pushed open the door to Tillie's shop and stepped inside. She stopped just past the door frame. *The shop usually doesn't look like this!* she thought. Tutus were flung everywhere. Ribbons and bows were piled tail high. Bolts of cloth crisscrossed the room.

What was going on?

Sultan sniffed the air. "Something's not right," he said.

Dreamy heard a noise. Her ears twitched. It sounded like a mouse squeak. Or a very sad little kitten.

"This way," Dreamy whispered to Pumpkin and Sultan. She followed the sound to the far corner of the shop. Soft sobs were coming from a pile of cloth. Dreamy pulled aside a bolt of fabric.

There, on a pile of tutus, sat Tillie.

The little kitten wiped a tear from her whiskers.

"What's wrong?" Pumpkin asked.

"Everything!" Tillie let out a sob. "I'm making the costumes for the *Midsummer Night's Dream* show. And I have no new ideas." She raised a paw dramatically to her head. "My inspiration," she cried. "It's gone!"

"I'll find it!" Sultan dashed away to search the shop. A moment later, he slunk back. "Oh," he said. "I forgot. You can't really find inspiration that way, can you?"

"Nope," Pumpkin said.

"Inspiration isn't something you can touch, like a ball or a kitty bed," Dreamy said. "It's more like . . . a dream." Yes, that was it. Inspiration was like a dream.

"Thanks for looking anyway," Tillie added with a sniffle.

Dreamy hated to see the tailor kitty so sad. "What happened?" she asked.

"I was so excited to work on the costumes," Tillie explained. "I sat down with my crayons and paper. And a cup of tuna tea. That's how I work best."

Dreamy nodded. Tuna tea was very inspiring!

"Usually I have lots of ideas," Tillie went on. "But this time, nothing! Not a single thread of a theme. Not a scrap of an idea. Not even a knot of a notion."

"Have you tried a nap?" Dreamy asked.

Tillie shook her head. "I don't have time. The show is in two weeks!"

Poor Tillie! Dreamy tried to imagine suddenly not being able to sleep. She shuddered. It would be tragic!

Dreamy batted at a piece of fabric. Maybe she could help Tillie. She pushed at the cloth with her paws. Dreamy didn't know much about costumes.

"It's been days!" Tillie said. "What will I do if I can't come up with—" Then she stopped. Her green cat eyes widened. She looked at the fabric Dreamy had been toying with. Dreamy looked down at it, too. She had kneaded it into even folds.

"Oops," Dreamy said. She turned pinker than usual. "Sorry! I didn't mean to wrinkle it."

"Sorry? Don't be sorry." Tillie snatched up the fabric. "It's perfect! Pleats!" she exclaimed.

Tillie twirled around the shop with the pleated fabric in her paws. She twirled back to Pumpkin, Sultan, and Dreamy. They watched her, openmouthed.

"I've found my inspiration!" Tillie said. "Dreamy, it's YOU!"

"Sky blue or sea blue?" Tillie held up two swatches of fabric.

Sky blue or sea blue? What was the difference? Dreamy could hardly tell. She needed a nap. But napping at Tillie's Tutu Tailor Shop was impossible. Tillie talked nonstop!

At first, Dreamy had been thrilled to

help Tillie. It was fun to be her inspiration. Ribbon or roses? Silk or satin? Baubles or beads? But she'd spent two hours looking at colors, patterns, cloth, and trim. She felt super sleepy!

Should she say something? But Tillie looked so happy. Dreamy didn't want to make her sad again.

Dreamy waved a paw at a random swatch.

"Sky blue! Of course," Tillie said. "Now, what do you think—polka dots or stripes?"

"I think . . . I need to go home," Dreamy said. Sultan had gone off to Mr. Chow's.

And Pumpkin had left more than an hour

before, the lucky dog.

"Yes!" Tillie said. "I'll come with you!"

Dreamy sighed. She would never get

her nap now!

Tillie picked up her sketch pad, a bag

of fabric, and a pincushion filled with

needles. She dropped them all into a bag to bring along.

At the door of the shop, Tillie flipped her sign from OPEN to CLOSED. "Who knows when I'll be back?" she said with a laugh.

Dreamy didn't laugh.

CLOSED

A
Midsummer
Night's
Dream

She was too tired. But she did her best not to let Tillie see.

Tillie trotted beside Dreamy on the path to the Pawlace.

"It's such a wonderful show," she said. "With you as my inspiration, we'll make beautiful costumes!"

Dreamy yawned. Then something caught her eye. Next to the path stood the Whisker Haven Playhouse. Critterzens and Palace Pets had gathered in front of it.

Tillie followed her gaze. "Oh! That must be the tryouts!"

"Dreamy! Dreamy!" Pumpkin came running toward them at full speed. She launched herself at Dreamy, and the two pets tumbled across the grass.

"Guess what!" Pumpkin said when they came to a stop. "I'm in the show! And so are Sultan and Petite and Berry and Treasure!"

Pumpkin jumped to her paws and twirled happily. Dreamy didn't. The grass was soft, like a feather bed. Or a marshmallow. Her eyes drifted shut.

A soft tap woke her. Lucy the wiener puppy smiled down at her. She held a

clipboard in her paws. "Want to be in the show, too?" she asked. "You could be a fairy!"

A fairy? That sounded dreamy! "All right," Dreamy purred.

Pumpkin barked. "Hooray! Dreamy will be in the show!"

Tillie clapped her hands together. "What fun!" she said. "You can practice for the show *and* be my inspiration!"

Dreamy's eyes grew wide. She had to do both? Be in the show? *And* be Tillie's inspiration? "But what—what about *sleep*?" she asked.

Tillie shrugged. "Who needs sleep?"

Me! Dreamy thought. But she didn't say it out loud. She didn't want to hurt Tillie's feelings.

Tillie went on. "I once worked forty-eight hours straight. All I need is the right inspiration!" She got down to ground level. The two kittens eyed each other. "And you, Dreamy, are very inspiring!"

Dreamy frowned. She didn't want to be anyone's inspiration anymore!

"This is the best," Tillie mumbled through the pins in her mouth. "You are my muse"—she folded over a seam and secured it with a pin—"but you're my model, as well!"

Dreamy stood on a wooden fruit crate while lilac fabric was wrapped around her. Tillie was fitting her latest costume . . . on Dreamy!

In the two weeks since tryouts, Tillie had been Dreamy's constant shadow. Most of the time, Tillie worked on costumes. And Dreamy? Most of the time, *she* just tried to sneak in a nap!

A frayed edge of the fabric tickled Dreamy's nose. She blew on it. It shifted, but only for a moment. Dreamy raised her paw to swat it away—

"Careful!" Tillie said. "This dress is delicate."

Dreamy lowered her paw and yawned. Her eyes closed for a second. She felt herself sway, so she opened them again.

If she didn't watch out, she'd topple off the fruit crate!

Berry poked her head into the room. "I brought a snack." She held out a plate of cranberry branberries.

"Can I have one?" Sultan joined the gray bunny at the door. He was trailed by Pumpkin and Petite.

Dreamy smiled. Whenever Berry baked, she had followers!

Tillie waved. "Can't stop to snack. The show's tomorrow!"

"Take a nap, Tillie," Dreamy suggested. "I always feel better afterward."

The tailor kitten shook her head. She grabbed her scissors and cut the dress shorter.

"We were practicing," Petite told Tillie and Dreamy.

Dreamy rubbed her nose with her

paw. She wished she could practice now, too. It was almost as much fun as napping!

"We'll show you!" Pumpkin said. Tillie opened her mouth, but Pumpkin hushed her. "You can listen and work at the same time."

Pumpkin leaned back on her paws. She breathed in deeply. She closed her eyes.

"That's how she prepares," Petite whispered.

Pumpkin's eyes popped open. "'What fools these mortals be,'" she said.

Sultan stepped forward and spoke

the next line. "'Stand aside,'" he growled, "'the noise they make . . .'"

"'. . . will cause *Dreamy* to awake'!" Petite, Pumpkin, and Berry joined in on the last line.

"Hooray!" Tillie and Dreamy cheered.

"We don't say 'Dreamy' in the play," Pumpkin confessed. "We added that part. You know, because you're always sleeping."

Not anymore! poor Dreamy thought grumpily.

"It was wonderful," Tillie said.

"*Purr*fect!" Dreamy agreed, clapping her paws together—

Riiiiiiiiip.

Dreamy heard the most awful tearing noise. She looked down. The side of the lilac dress had split wide open!

"Oops," Dreamy said with a wince.

"Oh, dear." Tillie grabbed the two seams and held them together. Threads stuck out in every direction. Tillie dropped the fabric and covered her eyes.

Dreamy felt awful. She hadn't meant to mess up the dress!

Tillie started pawing through her workbasket. Out flew a blue pincushion. Sultan ducked out of its way. The tailor

kitten tossed aside a big red button. It nearly bonked Petite on the nose!

"I'm sure I had some extra lilac

thread!" Tillie stopped. "Oh, I know! I left it in the other room." She darted out the door.

Dreamy hung her head. Some inspiration *she* was! Tillie was better off without her.

"Are you okay?" Berry asked.

"You looked tired," Petite said.

Sultan buffed his claws on his fur. "You know, now would be a good time for a nap," he suggested, looking at Dreamy from the corner of his eyes.

"A nap?" Dreamy perked up. A nap was exactly what she needed. "Yes!"

Petite whinnied. Sultan gave a happy roar.

"Go, kitty, go!" Pumpkin said.

Dreamy shed the dress. She left it in a heap on the crate, and then . . . she ran out of the room!

Dreamy dashed down the hallway. Where could she go for a catnap?

Not her bedroom. Tillie would find her before she fell asleep. Petite's library was an option. Or Sultan's Jungly Gym. Or . . .

Wait! She knew the perfect spot—Treasure's Under the Sea Playland! It was awfully wet from all the fountains. And the squirting fish, waterfalls, ponds, and streams. Tillie, like most cats, didn't like water. The Playland was the last place she would look.

Dreamy ran as fast as her paws would carry her. She arrived out of breath.

She found Treasure practicing for the play. When she saw Dreamy, she stopped. "Wha—"

Dreamy put a paw on Treasure's shoulder. "I need somewhere to hide!" she said.

"Hide?" Treasure's eyes brightened. She loved action, danger, and adventure! "You came to the right place!" She led

Dreamy to a rock outcropping. Treasure lifted a curtain of seaweed. Behind it was a cool, dark cave.

"It's perfect," Dreamy said, stepping inside.

Dreamy was alone in the dark. She turned in a circle and lay down. The cave floor wasn't soft like her kitten bed. But she didn't care.

Treasure gave Dreamy a little salute. She let the seaweed fall across the cave opening.

Dreamy fell asleep in seconds.

She dreamed she was a fairy kitten

with fairy kitten wings and a fairy kitten crown. She was sleeping on a bed of flowers. The air smelled like jasmine and roses—

"There you are!"

Dreamy's eyes shot open at the sound of Tillie's voice. Her dream vanished.

"I've been looking all over for you!" Tillie said. "Luckily, I saw this thread."

Lilac thread was wrapped around Tillie's left paw. "It's from the dress you tried on. I followed it through the Pawlace . . . straight to you!"

Dreamy's perfect nap, gone! Why couldn't Tillie find her own inspiration? If Tillie asked her for one more opinion, Dreamy was going to—

Tillie held up a pink skirt. "So, what do you think? Long or short?"

Long or short? Dreamy didn't care. She really didn't. She raked her claws across the bottom of the fabric. "Fringe," she said.

Tillie sat down and dropped the pink skirt into her lap. "Fringe," she said softly. "What a good idea."

Then Tillie looked around. She seemed to notice the cave for the first time. "Dreamy," she said, "were you *hiding* from me?" Her eyes widened. They filled with sadness.

Dreamy's heart lurched. "Hiding from you?" she echoed. "I . . ." Dreamy trailed off. The silence in the cave felt awkward. She hung her head. She had never wanted to hurt Tillie's feelings. But it looked like she had anyway.

"Yes," Dreamy admitted.

"Don't you like me?" Tillie asked.

"Of course I like you!" Dreamy said. "You're sweet and talented and so much fun to be around. But—I'm not like you. I can't stay awake working for hours. Just like you need to sew, I need to nap. And I couldn't do that when we were always together. So I *was* hiding from you. I'm sorry."

Tillie nodded, but the sadness was still there. "It's my fault. Making these costumes is my job. Not yours." She swallowed hard. "I just hope I can get them done by tomorrow."

Tillie left the cave. The pink skirt trailed limply behind her.

At last, Dreamy was alone. She could nap. But now she didn't want to anymore. She just wanted to make things right with Tillie.

Dreamy knocked on the door of Tillie's Tutu Tailor Shop. No one answered. She pushed it open. Inside, nothing had changed. The shop still looked like it had been hit by a whirlwind. In fact, the piles of tutus and ribbons looked like they had gotten bigger.

"Tillie?" Dreamy called. She didn't see the kitten anywhere.

"Over here," Tillie called.

Dreamy followed the voice to the back of the shop, where she found Tillie beside a huge pile of bows. Tillie's cap was crooked. Tea stains spotted her white skirt. Her fur stuck out in every direction.

Tillie didn't look up. The needle in her paws darted up and down, making neat stitches.

"I want to help," Dreamy said.

"Help?"

Dreamy nodded. "I don't want to be your muse. Or your inspiration," she said.

"But I do want to be your friend." She hoped Tillie still wanted that, too.

Tillie looked up. Tears filled her eyes. "Oh, Dreamy!" she said. "That means so much!" She put down the needle. "Can you hem those tutus over there? And then maybe sew some trim onto these tops? And after that . . ."

Dreamy sat down. Tillie showed her how to stitch a seam. Then Dreamy started to fix the tutu on top of the pile.

Day turned to night, and night soon turned to dawn. The two kittens worked nonstop, sewing and stitching and

hemming until their eyes were blurry.

Just after sunrise, Tillie fell asleep. Dreamy smiled. It was funny—Tillie was asleep, and Dreamy was awake! Dreamy was never the last one to go to sleep!

Tillie woke with a start. "I can't believe I fell asleep!" she said.

"I understand," Dreamy said. And she did, better than anyone. All kittens needed to nap—even Tillie.

Then Tillie clapped her paws together. "I had such a beautiful dream! I was riding a soft purple cloud full of sparkly stars. . . . Oh! That gives me the most wonderful idea for a new tutu! It's going to be my most beautiful creation yet!"

Hooray! Tillie's inspiration was back!

Later, Dreamy watched the sun set

through the shop windows. Tillie stitched on one last bead. She tied a knot. Then she used her kitten teeth to snap the thread. She stepped back to examine the finished piece.

"Done!" she said.

"We have to hurry," Dreamy said. "It's almost showtime!"

Dreamy and Tillie packed everything up and raced to the playhouse. They hung the costumes around the backstage area. The Critterzens and Palace Pets oohed and aahed when they saw what Tillie and Dreamy had created.

Everyone put on the costumes. Berry was every inch a fairy queen in her midnight-blue tutu and wings, and Sultan was a king. Petite looked like a lady in a flowing tunic. Pumpkin was a sprite named Puck. And Treasure wore the head of a donkey.

Dreamy sighed. "The costumes are wonderful!" she said.

"I have one more," Tillie said. She pulled a tutu from a bag. Sparkly silver stars dotted the soft purple fabric. "It's for you, Dreamy."

"For me?" It was the prettiest tutu Dreamy had ever seen! She put it on. Tillie fitted silver fairy kitten wings to Dreamy's back and placed a fairy kitten crown on her head. Then Dreamy and Tillie joined their friends on the stage.

Dreamy watched them proudly. Her friends were no longer horses and puppies, bunnies and kittens. Tillie's costumes had transformed them. They were kings and queens and fairies. They were magical.

Dreamy's heart swelled. She had helped make this magic happen. Knowing that she had played a role in it all felt better than even the best nap.

"'So good night,'" Pumpkin said, reciting the final lines of the play. "'Give me your paws if we be friends.'" She thrust her paw out dramatically.

Dreamy felt Tillie's paw in her paw.

"Friends," Tillie whispered. Dreamy nodded.

The crowd broke into applause. On the stage, the pets bowed. Someone threw confetti. The lights sparkled. The golden moon shone down on Whisker Haven.

It was just like a dream—a beautiful midsummer kitten's dream.

AFTERWORD

"I have had a most rare vision. I have had a dream."

A Midsummer Night's Dream is a real play. A man named William Shakespeare wrote it more than four hundred years ago. The story takes place in the woods, where three different groups roam— a troop of very silly actors, four young people from town, and a band of fairies.

It's one of Shakespeare's most famous plays, and it's still performed often.